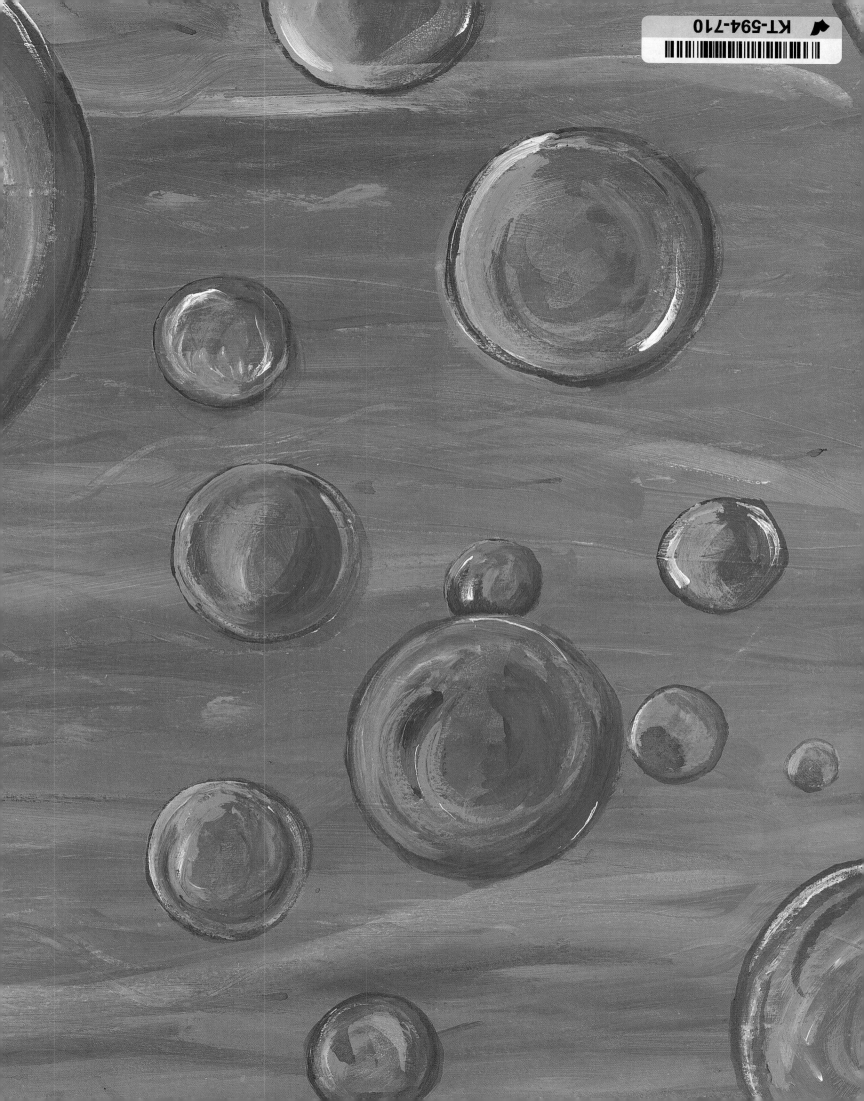

For Elaine, Joan, the Leigh Writers
and for Marion, without whom...
C.F.

To my grandads
S.J.

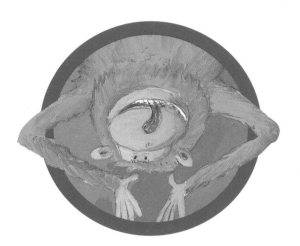

ORCHARD BOOKS
338 Euston Road, London NW1 3BH
Orchard Books Australia
Level 17/207 Kent Street, Sydney, NSW 2000

First published in 2001 by Orchard Books
First published in paperback in 2002
This edition published in 2010

ISBN 978 1 40830 809 7

Text © Claire Freedman 2001
Illustrations © Sean Julian 2001

The rights of Claire Freedman to be identified as the author and of Sean Julian to be identified as the illustrator
of this work have been asserted by them in accordance with the Copyright, Designs and Patents Act, 1988.

A CIP catalogue record for this book is available from the British Library.

1 3 5 7 9 10 8 6 4 2

Printed in China

Orchard Books is a division of Hachette Children's Books, an Hachette UK company.
www.hachette.co.uk

Where's Your Smile, CROCODILE?

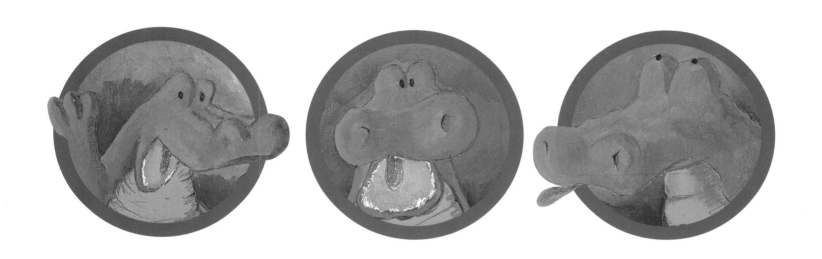

by Claire Freedman
illustrated by Sean Julian

ORCHARD BOOKS

One morning Kyle the Crocodile
woke up feeling very grumpy.
"Looks like you've lost your smile, Kyle,"
said Mum. "Why don't you go out and play?
You'll soon find it again."

So off Kyle trudged, through the
tangled jungle to Parrot's tree.
"Oh dear," Parrot squawked.
"Where's your smile, Crocodile?"
"I've lost it," said Kyle.
"Never mind," replied Parrot.
"I'll cheer you up with some of my
silly noises. You'll soon find it again."

SQUAWK! SCREECH!"
went Parrot as he whizzed
round and round on his branch.
All the animals who saw
laughed and laughed.
Ha ha ha!

But Kyle didn't laugh.
"My smile's not here," he said.
"It must be somewhere else."
And away he crawled to
look for it.

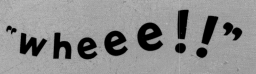

"wheee!!"
Suddenly down swung Orange Monkey.
"Oh dear, oh dear," he chattered.
"Where's your smile, Crocodile?"

"I've lost it," replied Kyle.
"Never mind," said Orange Monkey.
"You'll soon find it again. Why don't I cheer
you up with some of my funny faces?"

"YAHOO! YAHOO! YAHOO!" Orange Monkey pulled her mad face. . .

and her **CRAZY** face. . .

and her very funny hanging-upside-down-from-a-tree face.

All the animals who saw laughed and laughed.

Hee hee hee!

But Kyle didn't laugh. "My smile's not here," he said. "It must be somewhere else." And off he clomped down to the river bank to find it.

"Oh dear," Elephant trumpeted.
"Where's your smile, Crocodile?"
"I've lost it," sighed Kyle.

"Never mind," said Elephant. "You'll soon find it again. Watch me – I'll cheer you up."

Elephant blew big noisy bubbles in the water and squirted it everywhere. All the animals who saw laughed and laughed.

Ha ha ha!
Hee hee hee!

But Kyle didn't laugh.
"My smile's not here," he said.
"It must be somewhere else."
And away he plodded through the jungle creepers and lotus blossoms. . .

. . .where he found Little Lion Cub
sitting all by himself on an old termite hill.
   "Oh dear," said Kyle. "What ever is the matter?"
   "I've lost my way home!" Little Lion Cub sniffed.
   "And I've lost my smile," said Kyle.
"Shall we look for them together?"

So side by side they searched
through the jungle.

To cheer up Little Lion Cub
Kyle made some of Parrot's silly noises.

"SCREECH! SQUAWK! SCREECH!"

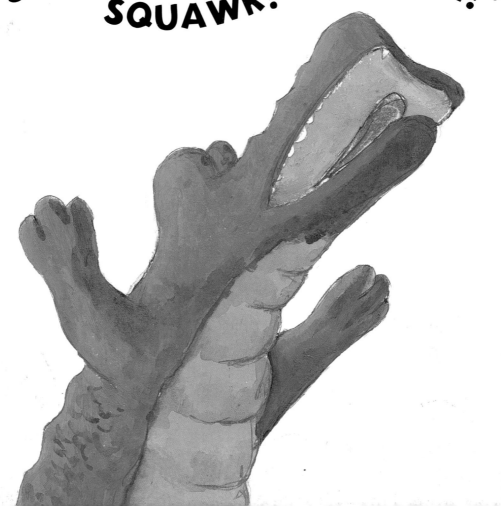

He pulled some funny
faces like Orange Monkey.

"YAHOO! YAHOO! YAHOO!"

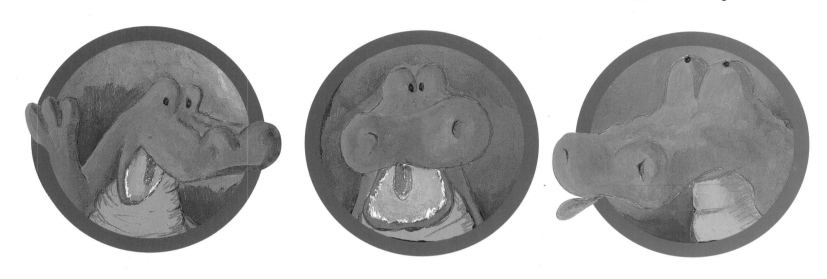

and blew big noisy bubbles in the water, like Elephant.

"BURBLE! BURBLE! BURBLE!"

Little Lion Cub soon felt happier.

As they reached the deep purple caves,
Little Lion Cub suddenly squealed.
"This is where I live! Thank you.
I've found the way home again."
"I'm glad I could help," said Kyle.
"And guess what?" said Little Lion Cub. . .

". . .you've found your smile, Kyle."
  "Have I?" said Kyle. "Where is it then?"
  "Back on your face,"
laughed Little Lion Cub,
"where it belongs!"

And so it was!

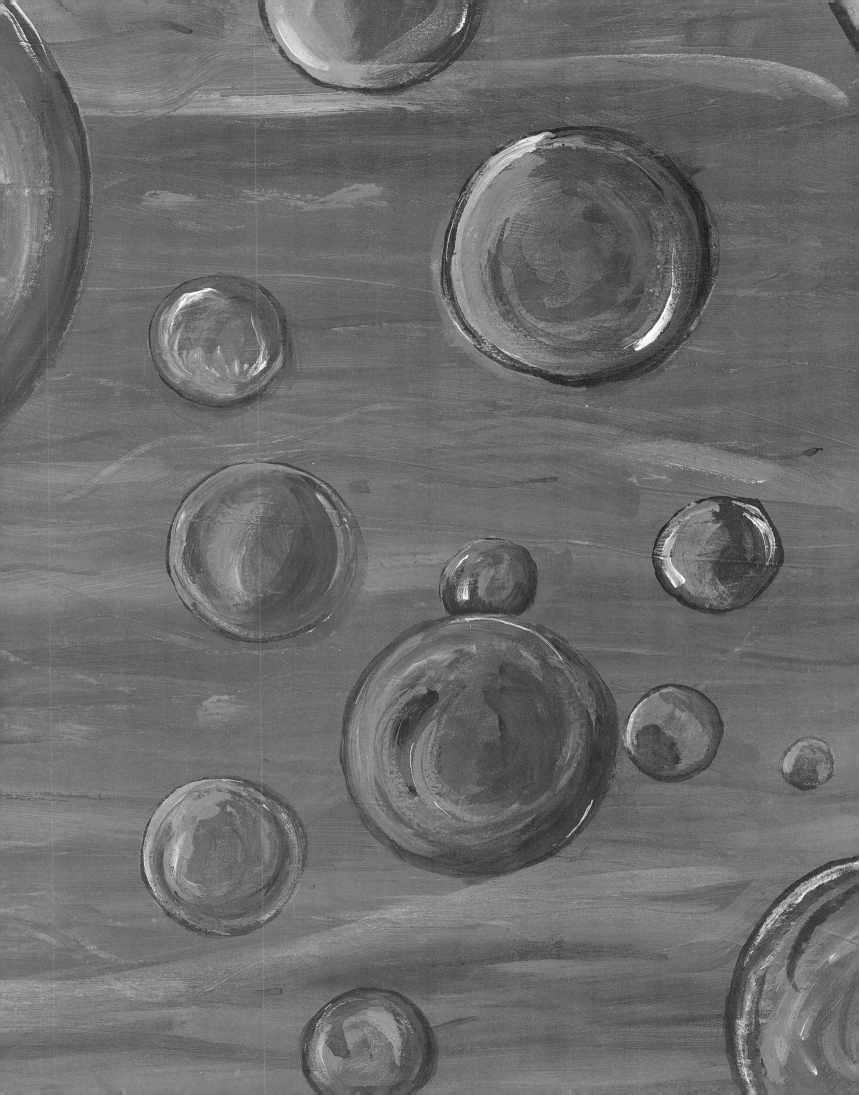